BUNNY CAKES

BUNNY CAKES

by
Rosemary Wells

PUFFIN BOOKS

For Ann Tobias

PUFFIN BOOKS
Published by the Penguin Group
Penguin Group (USA) LLC
375 Hudson Street
New York, New York 10014

USA * Canada * UK * Ireland * Australia
New Zealand * India * South Africa * China

penguin.com
A Penguin Random House Company
First published in the United States of America by Dial Books for Young Readers, a member of Penguin Putnam Inc., 1997
Published by Puffin Books, a member of Penguin Putnam Books for Young Readers, 2000

Copyright © 1997 by Rosemary Wells
All rights reserved

Penguin supports copyright. Copyright fuels creativity, encourages diverse voices, promotes free speech, and creates a vibrant culture. Thank you for buying an authorized edition of this book and for complying with copyright laws by not reproducing, scanning, or distributing any part of it in any form without permission. You are supporting writers and allowing Penguin to continue to publish books for every reader.

THE LIBRARY OF CONGRESS HAS CATALOGED THE DIAL EDITION AS FOLLOWS:
Wells, Rosemary.
Bunny cakes: a Max and Ruby picture book/Rosemary Wells. p. cm.
Summary: Max makes an earthworm cake for Grandma's birthday and helps Ruby with her angel surprise cake.
At the store, the grocer can't read all of the shopping list, until Max solves the problem by drawing a picture.
ISBN 0-8037-2143-9.
[1. Rabbits—Fiction. 2. Brothers and sisters—Fiction. 3. Baking—Fiction. 4. Cake—Fiction.] I. Title.
PZ7.W46843Bu 1997 [E]—dc20 95-52057 CIP AC

Puffin Books ISBN 978-0-14-056667-3

Printed in China

The artwork for each picture is an ink drawing with watercolor painting.

43 44 45 46 47 48 49 50

VISIT ROSEMARY WELLS AT www.rosemarywells.com

It was Grandma's birthday.

Max made her an earthworm birthday cake.

"No, Max," said Max's sister, Ruby. "We are going to make

Grandma an angel surprise cake with raspberry-fluff icing."

Max wanted to help.

"Don't touch anything, Max," said Ruby.

But it was too late.

Ruby sent Max to the store
with a list that said:

Max wanted Red-Hot Marshmallow Squirters for his earthworm cake. So he wrote "Red-Hot Marshmallow Squirters" on the list.

The grocer could not read Max's writing.

"Eggs!" said the grocer, and he gave Max eggs.

Max brought the eggs home to Ruby.

"Don't bump the table, Max!" said Ruby.

But it was too late.
Ruby sent Max back to the
store with a list that said:

This time Max wrote "Red-Hot Marshmallow Squirters"
in a different way.

Max hoped and hoped for his Squirters,

but the grocer still couldn't read Max's writing.

"Milk!" said the grocer, and he gave Max milk.

Max brought the milk home to Ruby.

"There's a yellow line on the floor, Max," said Ruby.

"You can't step over that line."

But Max crossed the line anyway.

Over went the flour.

Ruby got out her pencil.

This time Max wrote "Red-Hot Marshmallow Squirters"
in the most beautiful writing he knew.

Max could almost taste the Marshmallow Squirters.

"Flour," said the grocer, and he gave Max flour.

When Max got home, there was
a sign on the kitchen door.
"Max, the kitchen is no place
for you," said Ruby.

Ruby finished up her cake.

She baked it and cooled it and iced it
with raspberry-fluff frosting.
"It needs something else, Max," said Ruby.

"Birthday candles, silver stars, sugar hearts,
buttercream roses," wrote Ruby.
Meanwhile Max had a brand-new idea.

He drew a picture of Red-Hot
Marshmallow Squirters on
Ruby's list and ran to the grocer.
He could not wait.

"Birthday candles, silver stars, sugar hearts,
buttercream roses!" said the grocer. "What's this?
Why, it must be Red-Hot Marshmallow Squirters!"

Ruby's cake looked just beautiful.

Max went out and put caterpillar icing on his earthworm cake.

Grandma was so thrilled, she didn't know which cake to eat first.